Bannertail

Ernest Thompson Seton

Bannertail

CHAPTER I

THE FOUNDLING

IT was a rugged old tree standing sturdy and big among the slender second-growth. The woodmen had spared it because it was too gnarled and too difficult for them to handle. But the Woodpecker, and a host of wood-folk that look to the Woodpecker for lodgings, had marked and used it for many years. Its every cranny and borehole was inhabited by some quaint elfin of the woods; the biggest hollow of all, just below the first limb, had done duty for two families of the Flickers who first made it, and now was the homing hole of a mother Graysquirrel.

She appeared to have no mate; at least none was seen. No doubt the outlaw gunners could have told a tale, had they cared to admit that they went gunning in springtime; and now the widow was doing the best she could by her family in the big gnarled tree. All went well for a while, then one day, in haste maybe, she broke an old rule in Squirreldom; she climbed her nesting tree openly, instead of going up its neighbor, and then crossing to the den by way of the overhead branches. The farm boy who saw it, gave a little yelp of savage triumph; his caveman nature broke out. Clubs and stones were lying near, the whirling end of a stick picked off the mother Squirrel as she tried to escape with a little one in her mouth. Had he killed two dangerous enemies the boy could not have yelled louder. Then up the tree he climbed and found in the nest two living young ones. With these in his pocket he descended. When on the ground he found that one was dead, crushed in climbing down. Thus only one little Squirrel was left alive, only one of the family that he had seen, the harmless mother and two helpless, harmless little ones dead in his hands.

Why? What good did it do him to destroy all this beautiful wild life? He did not know. He did not think of it at all. He had yielded only to the wild ancestral instinct to kill, when came a chance to kill, for we must remember that when that instinct was implanted, wild animals were either terrible enemies or food that must be got at any price.

The excitement over, the boy looked at the helpless squirming thing in his hand, and a surge of remorse came on him. He could not feed it; it must die of hunger. He wished that he knew of some other nest into which he might put it. He drifted back to the barn. The mew of a young Kitten caught his ear. He went to the manger. Here was the old Cat with the one Kitten that had been left her of her brood born two days back. Remembrance of many Field-mice, Chipmunks and some Squirrels killed by that old green-eyed huntress, struck a painful note. Yes! No matter what he did, the old Cat would surely get, kill, and eat the orphan Squirrel.

Then he yielded to a sudden impulse and said: "Here it is, eat it now." He dropped the little stranger into the nest beside the Kitten. The Cat turned toward it, smelled it suspiciously once or twice, then licked its back, picked it up in her mouth, and tucked it under her arm, where half an hour later the boy found it taking dinner alongside its new-found foster-brother, while the motherly old Cat leaned back with chin in air, half-closed eyes and purring the happy, contented purr of mother pride. Now, indeed, the future of the Foundling was assured.

CHAPTER II

HIS KITTENHOOD

ITTLE Graycoat developed much faster than his Kitten foster-brother. The spirit of play was rampant in him, he would scramble up his mother's leg a score of times a day, clinging on with teeth, arms and claws, then mount her back and frisk along to climb her upright tail; and when his weight was too much, down the tail would droop, and he would go merrily sliding off the tip to rush to her legs and climb and toboggan off again. The Kitten never learned the trick. But it seemed to amuse the Cat almost as much as it did the Squirrelet, and she showed an amazing partiality for the lively, long-tailed Foundling. So did others of importance, men and women folk of the farmhouse, and neighbors too. The frisky Graycoat grew up amid experiences foreign to his tastes, and of a kind unknown to his race.

The Kitten too grew up, and in midsummer was carried off to a distant farmhouse to be "their cat."

Now the Squirrel was over half-grown, and his tail was broadening out into a great banner of buff with silver tips. His life was with the old Cat; his food was partly from her dish. But many things there were to eat that delighted him, and that pleased her not. There was corn in the barn, and chicken-feed in the yard, and fruit in the garden. Well-fed and protected, he grew big and handsome, bigger and handsomer than his wild brothers, so the house-folk said. But of that he knew nothing; he had never seen his own people. The memory of his mother had faded out. So far as he knew, he was only a bushy-tailed Cat. But inside was an inheritance of instincts, as well as of blood and bone, that would surely take control and send him herding, if they happened near, with those and those alone of the blowsy silver tails.

CHAPTER III

THE RED HORROR

N the Hunting-moon it came, just when the corn begins to turn, and in the dawn, when Bannertail Graycoat was yielding to the thrill that comes with action, youth and life, in dew-time.

There was a growing, murmuring sound, then smoke from the barn, like that he had seen coming from the red mystery in the cook-house. But this grew very fast and huge; men came running, horses frantically plunging hurried out, and other living things and doings that he did not understand. Then when the sun was high a blackened smoking pile there was where once had stood the dear old barn; and a new strange feeling over all. The old Cat disappeared. A few days more and the house-folk, too, were gone. The place was deserted, himself a wildwood roving Squirrel, quite alone, without a trace of Squirrel training, such as example of the old ones gives, unequipped, unaccompanied, unprepared for the life-fight, except that he had a perfect body, and in his soul enthroned, the many deep and dominating instincts of his race.

CHAPTER IV

THE NEW AND LONELY LIFE

HE break was made complete by the Red Horror, and the going of the man-people. Fences and buildings are good for some things, but the tall timber of the distant wooded hill was calling to him and though he came back many a time to the garden while there yet was fruit, and to the field while the corn was standing, he was ever more in the timber and less in the open.

Food there was in abundance now, for it was early autumn; and who was to be his guide in this: "What to eat, what to let alone?" These two guides he had, and they proved enough: instinct, the wisdom inherited from his forebears, and his keen, discriminatingnose.

Scrambling up a rotten stub one day, a flake of bark fell off, and here a-row were three white grubs; fat, rounded, juicy. It was instinct bade him seize them, and it was smell that justified the order; then which, it is hard to say, told him to reject the strong brown nippers at one end of each prize. That day he learned to pry off flakes of bark for the rich foodstuffs lodged behind.

At another time, when he worked off a slab of bark in hopes of a meal, he found only a long brown millipede. Its smell was earthy but strange, its many legs and its warning feelers, uncanny. The smell-guide seemed in doubt, but the inborn warden said: "Beware, touch it not." He hung back watching askance, as the evil thing, distilling its strange pestilent gas, wormed Snake-like out of sight, and Bannertail in a moment had formed a habit that was of his race, and that lasted all his life. Yea, longer, for he passed it on—this: Let the hundred-leggers alone. Are they not of a fearsome poison race?

Thus he grew daily in the ways of woodlore. He learned that the gum-drops on the wounded bark of the black birch are good to eat, and the little faded brown umbrella in the woods is the sign that it has a white cucumber in its underground cellar; that the wild bees' nests have honey in them, and grubs as good as honey; but beware, for the bee has a sting! He learned that the little rag-bundle babies hanging from vine and twig, contain some sort of a mushy shell-covered creature that is amazingly good to eat; that the little green apples that grow on the oaks are not acorns, and are yet toothsome morsels of the lighter sort, while nearly every bush in the woods atautumn now had strings of berries whose pulp was good to eat and whose single inside seed was as sweet as any nut. Thus he was learning woodcraft, and grew and prospered, for outside of sundry Redsquirrels and Chipmunks there were few competitors for this generous giving of the Woods.

CHAPTER V

THE FLUFFING OF HIS TAIL

HERE are certain stages of growth that are marked by changes which, if not sudden, are for a time very quick, and the big change in Bannertail, which took place just as he gave up the tricks and habits learned from his Cat-folk, and began to be truly a Squirrel, was marked by the fluffing of his tail. Always long and long-haired, it was a poor wisp of a thing until the coming of the Hunting-moon. Then the hairs grew out longer and became plumy, then the tail muscles swelled and worked with power. Then, too, he began a habit of fluffing out that full and flaunting plume every few minutes. Once or twice a day he combed it, and ever he was most careful to keep it out of wet or dirt. His coat might be stained with juice of fruit or gum of pine, and little he cared; but the moment a pine drop or a bit of stick, moss, or mud clung to his tail he stopped all other work to lick, clean, comb, shake, fluff and double-fluff that precious, beautiful member to its perfect fulness, lightness, and plumy breadth.

Why? What the trunk is to the elephant and the paw to the monkey, the tail is to the Graysquirrel. It is his special gift, a vital part of his outfit, the secret of his life. The 'possum's tail is to swing by, the fox's tail for a blanket wrap, but the Squirrel's tail is a parachute, a "land-easy"; with that in perfect trim he can fall from any height in any tree and be sure of this, that he will land with ease and lightness, and on his feet.

This thing Bannertail knew without learning it. It was implanted, not by what he saw in Kitten days, or in the woods about, but by the great All-Mother, who had builded up his athlete form and blessed him with an inner Guide.

CHAPTER VI

THE FIRST NUT CROP

HAT year the nut crop was a failure. This was the off-year for the red oaks; they bear only every other season. The white oaks had been nipped by a late frost. The beech-trees were very scarce, and the chestnuts were gone — the blight had taken them all. Pignut hickories were not plentiful, and the very best of all, the sweet shag-hickory, had suffered like the white oaks.

October, the time of the nut harvest, came. Dry leaves were drifting to the ground, and occasional "thumps" told of big fat nuts that also were falling, sometimes of themselves and sometimes cut by harvesters; for, although no other Graysquirrel was to be seen, Bannertail was not alone. A pair of Redsquirrels was there and half a dozen Chipmunks searching about for the scattering precious nuts.

Their methods were very different from those of the Graysquirrel race. The Chipmunks were carrying off the prizes in their cheek-pouches to underground storehouses. The Redsquirrels were hurrying away with their loads to distant hollow trees, a day's gathering in one tree. The Graysquirrels' way is different. With them each nut is buried in the ground, three or four inches deep, one nut at each place. A very precise essential instinct it is that regulates this plan. It is inwrought with the very making of the Graysquirrel race. Yet in Bannertail it was scarcely functioning at all. Even the strongest inherited habit needs a starter.

How does a young chicken learn to peck? It has a strong inborn readiness to do it, but we know that that impulse must be stimulated at first by seeing the mother peck, or it will not function. In an incubator it is necessary to have a sophisticated chicken as a leader, or the chickens of the machine foster-mother will die, not knowing how to feed. Nevertheless, the instinct is so strong that a trifle will arouse it to take control. Yes, so small a trifle as tapping on the incubator floor with a pencil-point will tear the flimsy veil, break the restraining bond and set the life-preserving instinct free.

Like this chicken, robbed of its birthright by interfering man, was Bannertail in his blind yielding to a vague desire to hide the nuts. He had never seen it done, the example of the other nut-gatherers was not helpful—was bewildering, indeed.

Confused between the inborn impulse and the outside stimulus of example, Bannertail would seize a nut, strip off the husk, and hide it quickly anywhere. Some nuts he would thrust under bits of brush or tufts of grass; some he buried by dropping leaves and rubbish over them, and a few, toward the end, he hid by digging a shallow hole. But the real, well-directed, energetic instinct to hide nut after nut, burying them three good inches, an arm's length, underground, was far from being aroused, was even hindered by seeing the Redsquirrels and the Chipmunks about him bearing away their stores, without attempting to bury them at all.

So the poor, skimpy harvest was gathered. What was not carried off was hidden by the trees themselves under a layer of dead and fallen leaves.

High above, in an old red oak, Bannertail found a place where a broken limb had let the weather in, so the tree was rotted. Digging out the soft wood left an ample cave, which he gnawed and garnished into a warm and weather-proof home.

The bright, sharp days of autumn passed. The leaves were on the ground throughout the woods in noisy dryness and lavish superabundance. The summer birds had gone, and the Chipmunk, oversensitive to the crispness of the mornings, had bowed sedately on November 1, had said his last "good-by," and had gone to sleep. Thus one more voice was hushed, the feeling of the woods was "Hush, be still!"—was all-expectant of some new event, that the tentacles of high-strung wood-folk sensed and appraised as sinister. Backward they shrank, to hide away and wait.

CHAPTER VII

THE SUN SONG OF BANNERTAIL

HE sun was rising in a rosy mist, and glinting the dew-wet overlimbs, as there rang across the bright bare stretch of woodland a loud "Qua, qua, qua, quaaaaaaa!" Like a high priest of the sun on the topmost peak of the temple stood Bannertail, carried away by a new-born inner urge. A full-grown wildwood Graysquirrel he was now, the call of the woods had claimed him, and he hailed the glory of the east with an ever longer "Qua, qua, quaaaaaaaaaa!"

This was the season of the shortest days, though no snow had come as yet to cover the brown-leaved earth. Few birds were left of the summer merrymakers. The Crow, the Nuthatch, the Chickadee, and the Woodwale alone were there, and the sharp tang of the frost-bit air was holding back their sun-up calls. But Bannertail, a big Graysquirrel now, found gladness in the light, intensified, it seemed, by the very lateness of its coming.

"Qua, qua, qua, quaaaaaa," he sang, and done into speech of man the song said: "Hip, hip, hip, hurrahhh!"

He had risen from his bed in the hollow oak to meet and greet it. He was full of lusty life now, and daily better loved his life. "Qua, qua, qua, quaaaa!"—he poured it out again and again. The Chickadee quit his bug hunt for a moment to throw back his head and shout: "Me, too!" The Nuthatch, wrong end up, answered in a low, nasal tone: "Hear, hear, hear!" Even the sulky Crow joined in at last with a "'Rah, 'rah, 'rah!" and the Woodwale beat a long tattoo.

"Hip, hip, hip, hurrah, hurrah, hurrah!" shouted Bannertail as the all-blessed glory rose clear above the eastern trees and the world was aflood with the Sun-God's golden smile.

A score of times had he thus sung and whip-lashed his tail, and sung again, exulting, when far away, among the noises made by birds, was a low "Qua, quaaa!"—the voice of another Graysquirrel!

His kind was all too scarce in Jersey-land, and yet another would not necessarily be a friend; but in the delicate meaningful modulations of sound so accurately sensed by the Squirrel's keen ear, this far-off "Qua, qua," was a little softer than his own, a little higher-pitched, a little more gently modulated, and Bannertail knew without a moment's guessing. "Yes, it was a Graysquirrel, and it was not one that would take the war-path against him."

The distant voice replied no more, and Bannertail set about foraging for his morning meal.

The oak-tree in which he had slept was only one of the half-a-dozen beds he now claimed. It was a red oak, therefore its acorns were of poor quality; and it was on the edge of the woods. The best feeding-grounds were some distance away, but the road to them well known. Although so much at home in the trees, Bannertail travelled on the ground when going to a distance. Down the great trunk, across an open space to a stump, a pause on the stump to fluff his tail and look around, a few bounds to a fence, then along the top of that in three-foot hops till he came to the gap; six feet across this gap, and he took the flying leap with pride, remembering how, not so long ago, he used perforce to drop to the ground and amble to the other post. He was making for the white oak and hickory groves; but his keen nose brought him the message of a big red acorn under the leaves. He scratched it out and smelled it — yes, good. He ripped off the shell and here, ensconced in the middle, was a fat white grub, just as good as the nut itself, or better. So Bannertail had grub on the half-shell and nuts on the side for his first course. Then he set about nosing for hidden hickory-nuts; few and scarce were they. He had not found one when a growing racket announced the curse-beast of the woods, a self-hunting dog. Clatter, crash, among the dry leaves and brush, it came, yelping with noisy, senseless stupidity when it found a track that seemed faintly fresh. Bannertail went quietly up a near elm-tree, keeping the trunk between himself and the beast. From the elm he swung to a basswood, and finished his meal of basswood buds. Keeping one eye on the beast, he scrambled to an open platform nest that he had made a month ago, where he lazed in the sun, still keeping eyes and ears alert for tidings from the disturber below.

The huge brute prowled around and found the fresh scent up the elm, and barked at it, too, but of course he was barking up the wrong tree, and presently went off. Bannertail watched him with some faint amusement, then at last went rippling down the trunk and through the woods like a cork going down a rushing stream.

He was travelling homeward by the familiar route, on the ground, in undulated bounds, with pauses at each high lookout, when again the alarm of enemies reached him—a dog, sniffing and barking, and farther off a hunter. Bannertailmade for the nearest big tree, and up that he went, keeping ever the trunk between. Then came the dog—a Squirrel Hound— and found the track and yelped. Up near the top was a "dray," or platform nest, one Bannertail had used and partly built, and in this he stretched out contentedly, peering over the edge at the ugly brutes below. The dog kept yelping up the trunk, saying plainly: "Squirrel, squirrel, squirrel, up, up, up!" And the hunter came and craned his neck till it was cricked, but nothing he saw to shoot at. Then he did what a hunter often does. He sent a charge of shot through the nest that was in plain view. There were some heavy twigs in its make-up, and it rested on a massive fork, or the event might have gone hard with Bannertail. The timber received most of the shock of the shot, but a something went stinging through his ear tip that stuck beyond the rim. It hurt and scared him, and he was divided between the impulse to rush forth and seek other shelter, and the instinct to lie absolutely still. Fortunately he lay still, and the hunter passed on, leaving the Squirrel wiser in several ways, for now he knew the danger of the dray when gunners came and the wisdom of "lay low" when in doubt.

CHAPTER VIII

THE COLD SLEEP

EXT day there was a driving storm of snow, and whether the sun came up or not Bannertail did not know. He kept his nest, and, falling back on an ancient spend-time of the folk he kins with, he curled up into a sleep that deepened with the cold. This is partly a deliberate sleep. The animal voluntarily lets go, knowing that life outside is unattractive; he, by an act of the will, induces the cold sleep, that is like a chapter of forgetfulness, with neither hunger nor desire, and after it is over, no pain in punishment or remorse.

For two days the storm raged, and when the white flakes ceased to pile upon the hills and trees, a cutting blast arose that sent snow-horses riding across the fields and piled them up in drifts along the fences.

It made life harder for the Squirrel-Folk by hiding good Mother Earth from their hungry eyes; but in one way the wind served them, for it swept the snow from all the limbs that served the tree-folk as an over-way.

For two days the blizzard hissed. The third day it was very cold; on the fourth day Bannertail peeped forth on the changed white world. The wind, the pest of wild life in the trees, had ceased, the sky was clear, and the sun was shining in a weak, uncertain way. It evoked no enthusiasm in the Graycoat's soul. Not once did he utter his Sun-salute. He was stiff and sleepy, and a little hungry as he went forth. His hunger grew with the exercise of moving. Had he been capable of such thought he might have said: "Thank goodness the wind has swept the snow from the branches." He galloped and bounded from one high over-way to another, till a wide gap between tree-tops compelled him to descend. Over the broad forest floor of shining white he leaped, and made for the beloved hickory grove. Pine-cones furnish food, so do buds of elm and flower-buds of maple. Red acorns are bitter yet eatable, white acorns still better, and chestnuts and beechnuts delicious, but the crowning glory of a chosen feast is nuts of the big shag hickory—so hard of shell that only the strongest chisel teeth can reach them, so precious that nature locks them up in a strong-box of stone, enwrapped in a sole-leather case; so sought after, that none of them escape the hungry creatures of the wood for winter use, except such as they themselves have hidden for just such times. Bannertail quartered the surface of the snow among the silent bare-limbed trees, sniffing, sniffing, alert for the faintest whiff.

A hound would not have found it—his nose is trained for other game. Bannertail stopped, swung his keen "divining-rod," advanced a few hops, moved this way and that, then at the point of the most alluring whiff, he began to dig down, down through the snow.

Soon he was out of sight, for here the drift was nearly two feet deep. But he kept on, then his busy hind feet replacing the front ones as diggers for a time, sent flying out on the white surface brown leaves, then black loam. Nothing showed but his tail and little jets of leaf-mould. His whole arm's-length into the frosty ground did he dig, allured by an ever-growing rich aroma. At last he seized and dragged forth in his teeth a big fat hickory-nut, one buried by himself last fall, and, bounding with rippling tail up a tree to a safe perch that was man-high from the ground, he sawed the shell adroitly and feasted on the choicest food that is known to the Squirrel kind.

A second prowl and treasure-hunt produced another nut, a third produced an acorn, a visit to the familiar ever-unfrozen spring quenched his thirst, and then back he undulated through the woods and over the snow to his cosey castle in the oak.

CHAPTER IX

THE BALKING OF FIRE-EYES

THER days were much like this as the Snow-moon slowly passed. But one there was that claimed a place in his memory for long. He had gone farther afield to another grove of hickories, and was digging down so deep into the snow that caution compelled him to come out and look around at intervals. It was well he did so, for a flash of brown and white appeared on a near log. It made toward him, and Bannertail got an instinctive sense of fear. Small though it was, smaller than himself, the diabolic fire in its close-set eyes gave him a thrill of terror. He felt that his only safety lay in flight.

Now it was a race for the tall timber, and a close one, but Bannertail's hops were six feet long; his legs went faster than the eye could see. The deep snow was harder on him than on his ferocious enemy, but he reached the great rugged trunk of an oak, and up that, gaining a little. The Weasel followed close behind, up, up, to the topmost limbs, and out on a long, level branch to leap for the next tree. Bannertail could leap farther than Fire-eyes, but then he was heavier and had to leap from where the twigs were thicker. So Fire-eyes, having only half as far to go, covered the leap as well as the Squirrel did, and away they went as before.

Every wise Squirrel knows all the leaps in his woods, those which he can easily make, and those which will call for every ounce of power in his legs. The devilish pertinacity of the Weasel, still hard after him, compelled him to adopt a scheme. He made for a wide leap, the very limit of his powers, where the take-off was the end of a big broken branch, and racing six hops behind was the Brown Terror. Without a moment's pause went Bannertail easily across the six-foot gap, to land on a sturdy limb in the other tree. And the Weasel! He knew he could not make it, hung back an instant, gathered his legs under him, snarled, glared redder-eyed than ever, bobbed down a couple of times, measured the distance with his eye, then wheeled and, racing back, went down the tree, to cross and climb the one that sheltered the Squirrel. Bannertail quietly hopped to a higher perch, and, when the right time came, leaped back again to the stout oak bough. Again the Weasel, with dogged pertinacity, raced down and up, only to see the Graysquirrel again leap lightly across the impassable gulf. Most hunters would have given up now, but there is no end to the dogged stick-to-itiveness of the Weasel; besides, he was hungry. And half-a-dozen times he had made the long circuit while his intended victim took the short leap. Then Bannertail, gaining confidence, hit on a plan which, while it may have been meant for mere teasing, had all the effect of a deep stratagem played with absolute success.

When next the little red-eyed terror came racing along the oak limb, Bannertail waited till the very last moment, then leaped, grasped the far-side perch, and, turning, "yipped" out one derisive "grrrf, grrrf, grrrf" after another, and craned forward in mockery of the little fury. This was too much. Wild with rage, the Weasel took the leap, fell far short, and went whirling head over heels down seventy-five feet, to land not in the soft snow but on a hard-oak log, that knocked out his cruel wind, and ended for the day all further wish to murder or destroy.

CHAPTER X

REDSQUIRREL, THE SCOLD OF THE WOODS

HE Snow-moon was waning, the Hunger-moon at hand, when Bannertail met with another adventure. He had gone far off to the pine woods of a deep glen, searching for cones, when he was set on by a Redsquirrel. Flouncing over the plumy boughs it came, chattering: "Squat, squat, quit, quit, quit" — "git, git, git" — and each moment seemed more inclined to make a tooth-and-nail attack on Bannertail. And he, what had he to fear? Was he not bigger and stronger than the Red-headed One? Yes, very well able to overmatch him in fight, but his position was much like that of a grown man who is assailed by a blackguard boy. There is no glory in the fight, if it comes to that. There is much unpleasant publicity, and the man usually decides that it is better to ignore the insult and retreat. This was Bannertail's position exactly. He hated a row — most wild things do — it brings them into notice of the very creatures they wish to avoid. Besides, the Redsquirrel was not without some justification, for these were his pine-trees by right of long possession. Bannertail, without touch of violence or fear of it, yielded to the inward impulses, yielded and retreated, closely pursued by the Redsquirrel, who kept just out of reach, but worked himself up into a still noisier rage as he saw the invader draw off. It was characteristic of the Red One that he did not stop at the border of his own range but followed right into the hickory country, shrieking: "Git, git, ye brute ye, ye brute ye, git!" with insolence born of his success, though its real explanation was beyond him.

CHAPTER XI

BANNERTAIL AND THE ECHO VOICE

HE Hunger-moon, our February, was half worn away when again the sky gods seemed to win against the powers of chill and gloom. Food was ever scarcer, but Bannertail had enough, and was filled with the vigor of young life. The sun came up in a cloudless sky that day, and blazed through the branches of still, tense woodland, the air was crisp and exhilarating, and Bannertail, tingling with the elation of life, leaped up for the lust of leaping, and sang out his loudest song:

"Qua, qua, qua, quaaaaaaaaaaaaaaaaaaa!" from a high perch. Ringing across the woodland it went, and the Woodwales drummed on hardwood drums, in keen responsiveness, to the same fair, vernal influence of the time.

Though he seemed only to sing for singing's sake, he was conscious lately of a growing loneliness, a hankering for company that had never possessed him all winter; indeed, he had resented it when any hint of visitors had reached him, but now he was restless and desireful, as well as bursting with the wish to sing.

"Qua, qua, qua, quaaaaaaaaaaaaaaaaaa!" he sang again and again, and on the still, bright air were echoes from the hills.

"Qua, qua, quaaaaaaaaaaaaaaaa!" He poured it out again, and the echo came, "Qua, quaaaaa!" Then another call, and the echo, "Quaaa!"

Was it an echo?

He waited in silence—then far away he heard the soft "Qua, quaa" that had caught his ear last fall. The voice of another Graycoat, but so soft and alluring that it thrilled him. Here, indeed, was the answer to the hankering in his heart.

But even as he craned and strained to locate its very place, another call was heard:

"Qua, qua, qua, quaaaaaaa"

from some big strong Graycoat like himself, and all the fighting blood in him was stirred. He raced to the ground and across the woodland to the hillside whence the voice came.

On a log he stopped, with senses alert for new guidance. "Qua, qua, quaaa," came the soft call, and up the tree went Bannertail, a silvery tail-tip flashed behind the trunk, and now, ablaze with watchfulness, he followed fast. Thencame a lone, long "Qua, qua," then a defiant "Grrff," like a scream, and a third big Graysquirrel appeared, to scramble up after Bannertail.

CHAPTER XII

THE COURTING OF SILVERGRAY

WAY went Silvergray, undulating among the high branches that led to the next tree, and keen behind came the two. Then they met at the branch that had furnished the footway for the Gray Lady, and in a moment they clinched. Grappling like cats, they drove their teeth into each other's shoulders, just where the hide was thickest and the danger least.

In their combat rage they paid no heed to where they were. Their every clutch was on each other, none for the branch, and over they tumbled into open space.

Two fighting cats so falling would have clutched the harder and hoped each that the other would be the one to land on the under side. Squirrels have a different way. Sensing the fall, at once they sprang apart, each fluffed his great flowing tail to the utmost — it is nature's own "land-easy" — they landed gently, wide apart, and quite unshaken even by the fall. Overhead was the Lady of the tourney, in plain view, and the two stout knights lost not a moment in darting up her tree; again they met on a narrow limb, again they clutched and stabbed each other with their chisel teeth, again the reckless grapple, clutch, and the drop in vacant air — again they shot apart, one landed on the solid ground, but the other — the echo voice — went splash, plunge into the deepest part of the creek! In ten heart-beats he was safely on the bank. But there is such soothing magic in cold water, such quenching of all fires, be they of smoke or love or war, that the Echo Singer crawled forth in quite a different mood, and Bannertail, flashing up the great tree trunk, went now alone.

To have conquered a rival is a long step toward victory, but it is not yet victory complete. When he swung from limb to limb, ever nearer the Silvergray, he was stirred with the wildest hankering of love. Was she not altogether lovely? But she fled away as though she feared him; and away he went pursuing.

There is no more exquisite climbing action than that of the Squirrel, and these two, half a leap apart, winding, wending, rippling through the high roof-tree of the woods, were less like two gray climbing things than some long, silvery serpent, sinuating, flashing in and out in undulating coils with endless grace and certainty among the trees.

Now who will say that Silvergray really raced her fastest, and who will deny that he did his best? He was strong and swift, the race must end, and then she faced him with anger and menace simulated in her face and pose. He approached too near; her chisel teeth closed on his neck. He held still, limp, absolutely unresisting. Her clutch relaxed. Had he not surrendered? They stood facing each other, an armed neutrality established, nothing more.

Shyly apart and yet together, they drifted about that day, feeding at feed time. But she was ready to warn him that his distance he must keep.

By countless little signs they understood each other, and when the night came she entered a familiar hollow tree and warned him to go home.

Next day they met again, and the next, for there is a rule of woodland courtship — three times he must offer and be refused. Having passed this proof, all may be well.

Thus the tradition of the woods was fully carried out, and Bannertail with Silvergray was looking for a home.

CHAPTER XIII

THE HOME IN THE HIGH HICKORY

ANNERTAIL was very well satisfied with the home in the red oak, and assumed that thither he should bring his bride. But he had not reckoned with certain big facts—that is, laws—for the reason that he had never before met them. The female wild thing claims all authority in matters of the home, and in the honeymoon time no wild mate would even challenge her right to rule.

So the red oak den was then and there abandoned. Search in the hickory grove resulted in a find. A Flicker had dug into the trunk of a tall hickory where it was dead. Once through the outer shell the inner wood was rotten punk, too easy for a Flicker to work in, but exactly right and easy for a Graysquirrel. Here, then, the two set to work digging out the soft rotten wood till the chamber was to their liking, much bigger than that the Woodpecker would have made.

March, the Wakening-moon, was spent in making the home and lining the nest. Bark strips, pine-needles, fine shreds of plants that had defied the wind and snow, rags of clothes left by winter woodmen, feathers, tufts of wool, and many twigs of basswood with their swollen buds, and slippery-elm, and one or two—yes, Silvergray could not resist the impulse—fat acorns found from last year's crop and hidden now deep in the lining of the nest. There can be no happier time for any wild and lusty live thing than when working with a loving mate at the building and making of the nest. Their world is one of joy—fine weather, fair hunting, with food enough, overwhelming instincts at their flush of compulsion—all gratified in sanest, fullest measure. This sure is joy, and Bannertail met each yellow sun-up with his loudest song of praise, as he watched it from the highest lookout of his home tree. His "qua" song reached afar, and in its vibrant note expressed the happy time, and expressing it, intensified it in himself. There seemed no ill to mar the time. Even the passing snow-storms of the month seemed trifles; they were little more than landmarks on the joyful way.

CHAPTER XIV

NEW RIVALS

HE stormy moon of March was nearly over when a change came on their happy comradeship. Silvergray seemed to beget a coolness, a singular aloofness. If they were on the same branch together she did not sit touching him. If he moved to where she chanced to stand, and tried, as a thousand times before, to snuggle up, she moved away. The cloud, whatever it was, grew bigger. In vain he sought by pleasing acts to win her back. She had definitely turned against him, and the climax came when one evening they climbed to their finished, set, and furnished house. She whisked in ahead of him, then, turning suddenly, filled the doorway with her countenance expressing defiance and hostility, her sharp teeth menacingly displayed. She said as plainly as she could: "You keep away; you are not wanted here."

And Bannertail, what could he do? Hurt, rebuffed, not wanted in the house he had made and loved, turned away perforce and glumly sought his bachelor home in the friendly old red oak.

Whatever was the cause, Bannertail knew that it was his part to keep away, at least to respond to her wishes. Next morning, after feeding, he swung to the nesting tree. Yes, there she was on a limb—but at once she retreated to the door and repeated the signal, "You are not wanted here." The next day it was the same. Then on the third day she was nowhere to be seen. Bannertail hung about hoping for a glimpse, but none he got. Cautiously, fearfully, he climbed the old familiar bark-way; silently arriving at the door, he gently thrust in his head. The sweet familiar furry smell told him "yes, she was there."

He moved inward another step. Yes, there she lay curled up and breathing. One step more; up she started with an angry little snort. Bannertail sprang back and away, but not before he had seen and sensed this solving of the mystery. There, snuggling together under her warm body were three tiny little baby Squirrels.

For this, indeed, it was that Mother Nature whispered messages and rules of conduct. For this time it was she had dowered this untutored little mother Squirrel with all the garnered wisdom of the folk before. Nor did she leave them now, but sent the very message to Mother Squirrel and Father Squirrel, and the little ones, too, at the very time when their own poor knowledge must have failed.

It was the unspoken hint from her that made the little mother-soon-to-be hide in the nesting-place some nuts with buds of slippery-elm, twigs of spice bush, and the bitter but nourishing red acorns. In them was food and tonic for the trying time. Water she could get near by, but even that called for no journey forth, it chanced that a driving rain drenched the tree, and at the very door she found enough to drink.

CHAPTER XV

BACHELOR LIFE AGAIN

ANNERTAIL was left to himself, like a bachelor driven to his club. He had become very wise in woodlore so that the food question was no longer serious. Not counting the remnant of the nuts still unearthed, the swelling buds of every sweet-sapped tree were wholesome, delicious food, the inner bark of sweet birch twigs was good, there were grubs and borers under flakes of bark, the pucker berries or red chokeberries that grow in the lowlands still hung in clusters. Their puckery sourness last fall had made all creatures let them alone, but a winter weathering had sweetened them, and now they were toothsome as well as abundant sustenance.

Another, wholly different food, was added to the list. With the bright spring days the yellow Sapsucker arrived from the South. He is a crafty bird and a lover of sweets. His plan is to drill with his sharp beak a hole deep through the bark of a sugar-maple, so the sap runs out and down the bark, lodging in the crevices; and not one but a score of trees he taps. Of course the sun evaporates the sap, so it becomes syrup, and even sugar on the edges. This attracts many spring insects, which get entangled in the sticky stuff, and the Sapsucker, going from tree to tree in the morning, feasts on a rich confection of candied bugs. But many other creatures of the woods delight in this primitive sweetmeat, and Bannertail did not hesitate to take it when he could find it. Although animals have some respect for property law among their own kind, might is the only right they own in dealing with others.

Amusement aplenty Bannertail found in building "drays," or tree nests. These are stick platforms of the simplest open-work, placed high in convenient trees. Some are for lookouts, some for sleeping-porches when the night is hot, some are for the sun-bath that every wise Squirrel takes. Here he would lie on his back in the morning sun with his belly exposed, his limbs outsprawling, and let the healing sun-rays strike through the thin skin, reaching every part with their actinic power.

Bannertail did it because it was pleasant, and he ceased doing it when it no longer pleased him. Is not this indeed Dame Nature's way? Pain is her protest against injury, and soothingness in the healthy creature is the proof that it is doing good. Many disorders we know are met or warded off by this sun-bath. We know it now. Not long ago we had no fuller information than had Bannertail on such things. We knew only that it felt good at the time and left us feeling better; so we took it, as he took it, when the need of the body called for it, and ceased as he did, when the body no longer desired it.

CHAPTER XVI

THE WARDEN MEETS AN INVADER

HE bond between them had kept Bannertail near his mate, and her warning kept him not too near. Yet it was his daily wont to come to the nesting tree and wait about, in case of anything, he knew not what. Thus it was that he heard a rustling in the near-by limbs one day, then caught a flash of red. A stranger approaching the tree of trees. All Bannertail's fighting blood was aroused. He leaped by well-known jumps, and coursed along well-known overways, till he was on the nesting tree, and undulated like a silvery shadow up the familiar trunk to find himself facing the very Redsquirrel whose range he once had entered and from whom he, Bannertail, had fled. But what a change of situation and of heart! Redhead scoffed and shook his flaming tail. He shrieked his "skit, skit" and stood prepared to fight. Did Bannertail hold back—he, Bannertail, that formerly had declined the combat with this very rogue? Not for an instant. There was new-engendered power within compelling him. He sprang on the Red bandit with all his vigor and drove his teeth in deep. The Redhead was a fighter, too. He clinched and bit. They clung, wrestled and stabbed, then, losing hold of the tree, went hurling to the earth below. In air they flung apart, but landing unhurt they clinched again on the ground; then the Redhead, bleeding from many little wounds, and over-matched, sought to escape, dodged this way and that, found refuge in a hole under a root; and Bannertail, breathless, with two or three slight stabs, swung slowly up the tree from which Silvergray had watched the fight of her mate.

There never yet was feminine heart that withheld its meed of worship from her fighting champion coming home victorious—which reason may not have entered into it at all. But this surely counted: The young ones' eyes were opened, they were no longer shapeless lumps of flesh. They were fuzzy little Squirrels. The time had come for the father to rejoin the brood.

With the come-together instinct that follows fight, he climbed to the very doorway; she met him there, whisker to whisker. She reached out and licked his wounded shoulder; when she reentered the den he came in too; nosing his brood to get their smell, just as a woman mother buries her nose in the creasy neck of her baby; he gently curled about them all, and the reunited family went sound asleep in their single double bed.

CHAPTER XVII

THE HOODOO ON THE HOME

OT many days later they had a new unfriendly visitor. It was in the morning rest hour that follows early breakfast. The familiarcluck, cluck of a Flicker had sounded from a near tree-top. Then his stirring tattoo was heard on a high dead limb of the one tree. A little later a scratching sound, and the hole above was darkened by the head and shoulders of a big bird peering down at them through the opening. His long, sharp beak was opened to utter a loud startling "clape!" Up leaped Bannertail to meet and fight off the invader. There was little fighting to be done, for the Flicker sprang back, and on to a high limb. His fighting feathers were raised, and his threatening beak did look very dangerous, but he did not wait for Bannertail to spring on him. He swooped away in a glory of yellow wings, and with a chuckle of derision. It was a small incident, but it made a second break in their sense of secrecy.

Then came another little shock. The Bluejay, the noisy mischief-maker, was prowling around the farmhouse, and high on a ledge he found a handful of big horse-chestnuts gathered by the boy "to throw at cats." Had he been hungry the Jay would have eaten them, but choice food was plentiful, so now his storage instincts took charge. The Bluejay nearly sprained his bill getting a hold on a nut, then carried it off, looking for a hollow tree in which to hide it, as is the custom of his kind. The hole he found was the Squirrel's nest. He meant to take a good look in before dropping it, but the nut was big and heavy, smooth and round. It slipped from his beak plump into the sleeping family, landing right on Bannertail's nose. Up he jumped with a snort and rushed to the door. The Bluejay was off at a safe distance, and chortled a loud "Tooral, tooral, jay, jay!" in mischievous mockery, then flew away. Bannertail might have taken that nut for a friendly gift, but its coming showed that the den was over-visible. There was something wrong with it.

Later the very same day, the Bluejay did this same thing with another big chestnut. Evidently now he enjoyed the commotion that followed the dropping of the nut.

One day later came a still more disturbing event. A roving, prowling cur found the fresh Squirrel track up the tree, and "yapped" so persistently that two boys who were leagued with the dog for all manner of evil, came, marked the hole and spent half an hour throwing stones at it, varying their volleys with heavy pounding on the trunk to "make the Squirrel come out."

Of course, neither Bannertail nor Silvergray did show themselves. That is very old wood-wisdom. "Lay low, keep out of sight when the foe is on the war-path." And at last the besiegers and their yap-colleague tramped away without having seen sign or hair of a Squirrel.

There was very little to the incident, but it sank deep into Silvergray's small brain. "This nest is ill-concealed. Every hostile creature finds it."

There was yet another circumstance that urged action. Shall I tell it? It is so unpicturesque. A Squirrel's nest is a breeding-ground for vermin; a nest that is lined with soft grass, feathers, and wool becomes a swarming hive. Bannertail's farm upbringing had made him all too familiar with feathers and wool. His contribution to the home furnishing had been of the kind that guaranteed a parasitic scourge. This thing he had not learned — for it is instilled by the smell of their mother nest — cedar bark and sassafras leaves, with their pungent oils, are needed to keep the irritating vermin swarm away. And Silvergray, was she at fault? Only in this, the purifying bark and leaves were scarce. She was weak compared with Bannertail. His contributions had so far outpointed hers that the nest had become unbearable. Their only course was to abandon it.

CHAPTER XVIII

THE NEW HOME

WICE a day now Silvergray left the little ones, to forage for herself, soon after sunrise and just before sunset. It was on the morning outing that she went house hunting. And Bannertail went too. Ever he led to the cosey home in his old red oak. But there is a right that is deeply rooted in custom, in logic, and in female instinct, that it is the she-one's privilege to select, prepare, and own the home. Every suggestion that he made by offered lead or actual entry, was scorned and the one who made it, snubbed. She did her own selecting, and, strangest thing of all, she chose the rude stick nest of a big-winged Hawk, abandoned now, for the Hawk himself, with his long-clawed mate, was nailed to the end of the barn.

Winter storm and beaming sun had purged and purified the rough old aerie; it was high on a most unclimbable tree, yet sheltered in the wood, and here Silvergray halted in her search. All about the nest and tree she climbed, and smelled to find the little owner marks, of musk or rasping teeth, if such there should be — the marks that would have warned her that this place was already possessed. But none there were. The place was without taint, bore only through and through the clean, sweet odor of the woods and wood.

And this is how she took possession: She rubbed her body on the rim of the nest, she nibbled off projecting twiglets, she climbed round and round the trunk below and above, thus leaving her foot and body scent everywhere about, then gathered a great mouthful of springtime twigs, with their soft green leaves, and laid them in the Hawk nest for the floor-cloth of her own.

She went farther, and found a sassafras, with its glorious flaming smell of incense, its redolence of aromatic purity, and with a little surge of joy instinctive she gathered bundle after bundle of the sweet, strong twigs, spread them out for the rug and matting of the house. And Bannertail did the same, and for a while they worked in harmony. Then was struck a harsh, discordant note.

Crossing the forest floor Bannertail found a rag, a mitten that some winter woodcutter had cast away, and, still obsessed with the nursery garnish of his own farm-kitten days, he pounced on this and bore it gleefully to the nest that they were abuilding. And Silvergray, what said she, as the evil thing was brought? She had no clear ideas, no logic from the other ill-starred home. She could not say: "There was hoodoo on it, and this ragged woollen mitt seems hoodoo-like to me." But these were her strange reactions. "The smell of that other nest was like this; that smell is linked with every evil memory. I do not want it here." Her instinct, the inherited wisdom of her forebears, indorsed this view, and as she sniffed and sniffed, the smell inspired her with intense hostility, a hostility that in the other nest was somewhat offset by the smell of her loved brood, but this was not—it was wholly strange and hostile. Her neck hair rose, her tail trembled a little, as, acting under the new and growing impulse of violent dislike, she hurled the offending rag far from the threshold of her nest. Flop it went to the ground below. And Bannertail, not quite understanding, believed this to be an accident. Down he went as fast as his fast feet could carry him, seized on the ragged mitten, brought it again to the home-building. But the instinct that had been slow arousing was now dominant in Silvergray. With an angry chatter she hurled the accursed thing afar, and made it clear by snort and act that "such things come not there."

This was the strenuous founding of the new nest, and these were among the hidden springs of action and of unshaped thoughts that ruled the founding.

The nest was finished in three days. A rain roof over all of fresh flat leaves, an inner lining of chewed cedar bark, an abundance of aromatic sassafras, one or two little quarrels over accidental rags that Bannertail still seemed to think worth while. But the new nest was finished, pure and sweet with a consecrating, plague-defying aroma of cedar and of sassafras to be its guardian angel.

CHAPTER XIX

THE MOVING OF THE YOUNG

T was very early in the morning, soon after sunrise, that they took the hazard of moving the young. Silvergray had fed the babies and looked out and about, and had come back and looked again. Then, picking up the nearest by the scruff of its neck, she rose to the doorway. Now a great racket sounded in the woods. Silvergray backed in again and down, dropped the young one, then put her head out. The noise increased, the trampling of heavy feet. She backed till only her nose was out, and watched. Soon there came in view huge red-and-white creatures with horns. She had often seen them, and held them harmless, but why were they moving so fast? There were other noises coming, much smaller, indeed, but oh, how much more dangerous were the two that followed and drove the herd!—a tow-topped boy and a yellow-coated dog. At war with all the world of harmless wood-folk, these two would leave a trail of slaughtered bodies in their wake, if only their weapons were as deadly as their wishes. So Silvergray sank back and brooded over the nursery, varying her loving mothering with violent scratching of a hind foot, or sudden pounce to capture with her teeth some shiny, tiny creeping thing among the bed stuff or on the young ones' fluffy skins.

The sun was up above the trees. The Bluejay sang "Too-root-el-too-root-el," which means, "all clear." And the glad Red Singing-Hawk was wheeling in great rhythmic swoops to the sound of his own wild note, "Kyo-kyo-kyoooo." He wheeled and rejoiced in his song and his flight.

"All's clear! All's well!" sang Crow and Bluejay—these watchful ones, watchful, perforce, because their ways of rapine have filled the world with enemies. And Silvergray prepared a second time for the perilous trip. She took the nearest of her babies, gently but firmly, and, scrambling to the door, paused to look and listen, then took the final plunge, went scurrying and scrambling down the trunk. On the ground she paused again, looked forward and back, then to the old nest to see her mate go in and come out again with a young one in his mouth, as though he knew exactly what was doing and how his help was needed. With an angry "Quare!" she turned and scrambled up again, bumping the baby she bore with many a needless jolt, and met Bannertail. Nothing less than rage was in her voice, "Quare, quare, quare!" and she sprang at him. He could not fail to understand. He dropped the baby on a broad, safe crotch, and whisked away to turn and gaze with immeasurable surprise. "Isn't that what you wanted, you hothead?" he seemed to say. "Didn't we plan to move the kids?" Her only answer was a hissing "Quare!" She rushed to the stranded little one, made one or two vain efforts to carry it, as well as the one already in her mouth, then bounded back to the old home with her own charge, dropped it, came rushing back for the second, took that home, too, then vented all her wrath and warnings in a loud, long "Qua!" which plainly meant: "You let the kids alone. I don't need your help. I wouldn't trust you. This is a mother's job."

She stayed and brooded over them a long time before making the third attempt. And this time the impulse came from the tickling crawlers in the bed. She looked forth, saw Bannertail sitting up high, utterly bewildered. She gave a great warning "Qua!" seized number one for the third time, and forth she leaped to make the great migration.

The wood was silent except for its own contented life, and she got half-way to the new nest, when high on a broad, safe perch she paused and set her burden down. Was it the maddening tickling of a crawler that gave the hint, or was it actual wisdom in the lobes behind those liquid eyes? Who knows? Only this is sure, she looked that baby over from end to end. She hunted out and seized in her teeth and ground to shreds ten of the plaguing crawlers. She combed herself, she scratched and searched her coat from head to tail, and on her neck, where she could not see, she combed and combed, till of this she was certain, no insects of the tickling, teasing kind were going with her to the new home. Then seizing her baby by the neck-scruff, up she bounded, and in ten heart-beats he was lying in their new and fragrant bed.

For a little while she cuddled him there, to "bait him to it," as the woodsmen say. Then, with a parting licking of his head, she quit the nest and hied away for the rest of the brood.

Bannertail had taken the hint. He was still up high, watching, but not going near the old nest.

Silvergray took number two and did the very same with him, deloused him thoroughly on the same old perch, then left him with the first. The third went through the same. And Silvergray was curled up with the three in the new high nest for long, before Bannertail, after much patient, watchful waiting, seeing no return of Silvergray, went swinging to the old nest to peep in, and realized that it was empty, cold, abandoned.

He sat and thought it over. On a high, sunny perch that he had often used, he made his toilet, as does every healthy Squirrel, thoroughly combed his coat and captured all, that is, one or two of the crawlers that had come from the old nest. He drank of the spring, went foraging for a while, then swung to the new-made nest and shyly, cautiously, dreading a rebuff, went slowly in. Yes, there they were. But would she take him in? He uttered the low, soft, coaxing "Er-er-er-er," which expresses every gentleness in the range of Squirrel thought and feeling. No answer. He made no move, but again gave a coaxing "Er-er-er," a long pause, then from the hovering furry form in the nest came one soft "Er," and Bannertail, without reserve, glided in and curled about them all.

CHAPTER XX

THE COMING-OUT PARTY

PRIL, the Green-grass Moon, was nearly gone, the Graycoats in their new high home were flourishing and growing. Happy and ed now, it was an event like a young girl's coming-out, when first these Squirrelets came forth from the nest "on their own," and crawling on their trembling legs, with watchful mother nigh. They one by one scrambled on to the roof of the home, and, with a general air of "Aren't we big; aren't we wonderful?" they stretched and basked in the bright warm morning sun.

A Hawk came wheeling high over the tree tops. He was not hunting, for he wheeled and whistled as he wheeled. Silvergray knew him well, and marked his ample wings. She had seen a Redtail raid. This might not be of the bandit kind, but a Hawk is a Hawk. She gave a low, warning "Chik, chik" to the family, to which they paid not a whit of attention. So she seized each in turn by the handy neck-scruff, and bundled him indoors to safety.

Three times this took place on different days. Three times the mother's vigorous lug home was needed, and by now the lesson was learned. "Chik, chik" meant "Look out; danger; get home."

They were growing fast now. Their coats were sleek and gray. Their tails were as yet poor skimps of things, but their paws were strong and their claws were sharp as need be. They could scramble all about the old Hawk nest and up and down the rugged bark of the near trunk. Their different dispositions began to show as well as their different gifts and make-up.

CHAPTER XXI

NURSERY DAYS OF THE YOUNG ONES

QUIRRELS do not name their babies as we do; they do not think of them by names; and yet each one is itself, has individual looks or ways that stand for that one in the mother's mind, so is in some sort its name. Thus the biggest one had a very brown head and a very gray coat. He was stronger than the others, could leap just a little farther and was not so ready to bite when playing with the rest. The second brother was not so big as Brownhead, and he had an impatient way of rebelling at any little thing that did not please him. He would explode into a shrill "Cray!" which was a well-known Squirrel exclamation, only he made it very thin and angry. Even to father and mother he would shriek "Cray!" if they did in the least a thing that was not to his wish.

The third and smallest was a little girl-Squirrel, very shy and gentle. She loved to be petted and would commonly snuggle up to mother, whining softly, "Nyek, nyek," even when her brothers were playing, as well as at feeding-time. So in this sort they named themselves, Brownhead, Cray, and Nyek-nyek.

The first lesson in all young wild life is this, "Do as you are told"; the penalty of disobedience is death, not always immediate, not clearly consequent, but soon or late it comes. This indeed is the law, driven home and clinched by ages of experience: "Obey or die."

If the family is outstretched in the sun, and keen-eyed mother sees a Hawk, she says, "Chik, chik," and the wise little ones come home. They obey and live. The rebellious one stays out, and the Hawk picks him up, a pleasant meal.

If the family is scrambling about the tree trunk and one attempts to climb a long, smooth stretch, from which the bark has fallen, mother cries "Chik, chik," warning that he is going into danger. The obedient one comes back and lives. The unruly one goes on. There is no clawhold on such trunks. He falls far to the ground and pays the price.

If one is being carried from a place of danger, and hangs limp and submissive from his mother's mouth, he is quickly landed in a place of safety. But one that struggles and rebels, may be cut by mother's tightening teeth, or dropped by her and seized on by some enemy at hand. There are always enemies alert for such a chance. Or if he swings to drink at the familiar spring and sees not what mother sees, a Blacksnake lurking on a log, or heeds not her sharp "Keep back," he goes, and maybe takes a single sip, but it is his last.

If one, misled by their bright color, persists in eating fruit of the deadly nightshade, ignoring mother's warning, "Quare, quare!" he eats, he has willed to eat; and there is a little Squirrel body tumbled from the nest next day, to claim the kindly care of growing plants and drifting leaves that will hide it from the view.

Yes, this is the law, older than the day when the sun gave birth to our earth that it might go its own way yet still be held in law: "Obey and live; rebel and die."

CHAPTER XXII

CRAY HUNTS FOR TROUBLE

OISTEROUS, strong, and merry was Brownhead, the very son of his father. Eager to do and ready to go; yet quick to hear when the warning came, "Quare," or the home call, "Chik, chik." Well-fleshed was he and deeply fur-clad, although it was scarcely mid-May, and his tail already was past the switch stage and was frilling out with the silver frill of his best kin. Frolicsome, merry, and shy, very shy was Nyek-nyek. In some speech she would have been styled a "mammy pet." Happy with mother, playing with her brothers, but ever ready to go to mother. Slight of body, but quick to move, quick to follow, and nervously quick to obey, she grew and learned the learning of her folk.

Last was Cray, quickest of them all, not so heavy as Brownhead, yet agile, inquisitive, full of energy, but a rebel all the time. He would climb that long, smooth column above the nest. His mother's warning held him not. And when the clawhold failed he slipped, but jumped and landed safe on a near limb.

He would go forth to investigate the loud trampling in the woods, and far below him watched with eager curiosity the big, two-legged thing that soon discovered him. Then there was a loud crack like a heavy limb broken by the wind, and the bark beside his head was splintered by a blow that almost stunned him with its shock, although it did not touch him. He barely escaped into the nest. Yes, he still escaped.

CHAPTER XXIII

THE LITTLE SQUIRRELS GO TO SCHOOL

HESE are among the lessons that a mother Squirrel, by example, teaches, and that in case of failure are emphasized by many little reproofs of voice, or even blows:

Clean your coat, and extra-clean your tail; fluff it out, try its trig suppleness, wave it, plume it, comb it, clean it; but ever remember it, for it is your beauty and your life.

When there is danger on the ground, such as the trampling of heavy feet, do not go to spy it out, but hide. If near a hole, pop in; if on a big high limb, lie flat and still as death. Do not go to it. Let it come to you, if it will.

In the air, if there is danger near, as from Hawks, do not stop until you have at least got into a dense thicket, or, better still, a hole.

If you find a nut when you are not hungry, bury it for future use. Nevertheless this lesson counted for but little now, as all last year's nuts were gone, and this year's far ahead.

If you must travel on the ground, stop every little while at some high place to look around, and fail not then each time to fluff and jerk your tail.

When in the distant limbs you see something that may be friend or foe, keep out of sight, but flirt your white tail tip in his view. If it be a Graycoat, it will answer with the same, the wigwag: "I'm a Squirrel, too."

Learn and practise, also, the far jumps from tree to tree. You'll surely need them some day. They are the only certain answer to the Red-eyed Fury that lives on Mice, but that can kill Squirrels, too, if he catches them; that climbs and jumps, but cannot jump so far as the Graycoats, and dare not fall from high, for he has no plumy tail, nothing but a useless little tag.

Drink twice a day from the running stream, never from the big pond in which the grinning Pike and mighty Snapper lie in wait. Go not in the heat of the day, for then the Blacksnake is lurking near, and quicker is he even than a Squirrel, on the ground.

Go not at dusk, for then the Fox and the Mink are astir. Go not by night, for then is the Owl on the war-path, silent as a shadow; he is far more to be feared than the swish-winged Hawk. Drink then at sunrise and before sunset, and ever from a solid log or stone which affords good footing for a needed sudden jump. And remember ever that safety is in the tree tops — in this and in lying low.

These were the lessons they slowly learned, not at any stated time or place, but each when the present doings gave it point. Brownhead was quick and learned almost overfast; and his tail responding to his daily care was worthy of a grown-up. Lithe, graceful Nyek-nyek too, was growing wood-wise. Cray was quick for a time. He would learn well at a new lesson, then, devising some method of his own, would go ahead and break the rules. His mother's warning "Quare" held him back not at all. And his father's onslaught with a nip of powerful teeth only stirred him to rebellious fight.

CHAPTER XXIV

THE LOPPING OF THE WAYWARD BRANCH

URIOSITY may be the trail to knowledge, but it skirts a dangerous cliff. The Rose moon, June, was on the hills, its thrill joy set the whole wood world joy-thrilling. The Bannertail family had frolicked in a game of tag-and-catch all around the old Hawk nest, and up the long smooth pole went Cray to show that he could do it. His mother warned him, "Quare!" but up he went, and down he came without a hint of failure. Then they scattered, scampering for a game of hide-and-seek, when the heavy sound of some big brute a-comingwas wind-borne to them. The mother gave the warning "Chik." Three of them quickly got to the safe old nest. Silvergray flattened on the up side of a rugged limb; Cray, seeing nothing near, and scoffing at their flurry, made for a big crotch into which he could sink from sight if need be, and waited. In vain his mother cried, "Chik"; Cray wouldn't "chik"; he wanted to know what it was all about. The heavy trampling sound came near. Silvergray peeped over and could see very well; it was the two-legged Brute with the yellow yapping four-legs that she more than once had met before. They rambled slashingly around; the Yap-cur eagerly wagging his hideous tail. He swung his black snout in the air, gave out a long "Yap!" another and another. Then the Two-legs came slowly nearer, staring up into the rooftrees and moving awkwardly sidewise round and round the tree. Cray peered out farther to watch him. In vain the wise little mother Squirrel whispered "Chik, chik!" No, he would not "chik." As the Ground-brute circled the tree, Cray, trying to keep him in sight, quit all attempt at hiding. The yellow four-legs yapped excitedly. Then the big Ground-brute held very still. Cray was amused at this; he felt so safe that he called out a derisive "Qua!" There was a loud sound like thunder, a flash like lightning, and Cray fell headlong, splashing the gold-green leaves with his bright, hot young blood. His mother saw him go with a clutching of her mother heart. And Mother Carey saw him go, and said: "It had to be." For this is the fulfilling of the law; this is the upbuilding of the race; this is the lopping of the wayward branch.

The big Ground-beast below seized on the quivering, warm young body, and yelled aloud: "Billy, Billee, I got him; a great big Silvergray! Yahoo!"

But the meaning of that was unknown to the little mother and the rest. They only knew that a huge, savage Brute had killed their little brother, and was filling the woods with its hideous blood-curdling roars.

CHAPTER XXV

BANNERTAIL FALLS INTO A SNARE

ANNERTAIL was now in fresh midsummer coat of sleekest gray. His tail was a silver plume, and bigger than himself. His health was perfect. And just so surely as a sick one longs to be and to stay at home, so a lusty Squirrel hankers to go a-roaming.

Swinging from tree to tree, leaping the familiar jump-ways, he left the family one early morning, drank deeply at the spring brook, went on aground "hoppity-hop" for a dozen hops, then stopped to look around and frisk his tail. Then on, and again a look around. So he left the hickory woods, and swung a mile away, till at last he was on the far hillside where first he met the Redhead.

High in a tasselled pine he climbed and sat, and his fine nose took in the pleasant gum smells with the zest that came from their strangeness as much as from their sweetness.

As he sat he heard a rustling, racketty little noise in the thicket near. Flattening to the bough and tightening in his tail he watched. What should appear but his old enemy, the Redhead, dragging, struggling with something on the ground, stopping to sputter out his energetic, angry "Snick, snick," as the thing he dragged caught in roots and twigs. Bannertail lay very low and watched intently. The Redsquirrel fussed and worked with his burden, now close at hand. Bannertail saw that it was a flat, round thing, like an acorn-cup, only many times larger, and reddish, with a big, thick stem on the wrong side—a stem that was white, like new-peeled wood.

Bannertail had seen such growing in the woods, once or twice; little ones they were, but his nose and his inner guide had said: "Let them alone." And here was this fiery little Redsquirrel dragging one off as though he had a prize! Sometimes he lifted it bodily and made good headway, sometimes it dragged and caught in the growing twigs. At last it got fixed between two,

and with the energy and fury that so often go with red hair, the Redhead
jerked, shoved, and heaved, and the brittle, red-topped toadstool broke in
two or three crisp pieces. As he sputtered and Squirrel-cussed, there was a
warning Bluejay note. Redhead ran up the nearest tree; as it happened, the
one in which was Bannertail, and in an instant the enemies were face to
face. "Scold and fight" is the Redsquirrel's first impulse, but when
Bannertail rose up to full height and spread his wondrous tail the Red one
was appalled. He knew his foe again; his keen, discriminating nose got
proofs of that. The memory of defeat was with him yet. He retreated, snick-
sputtering, and finally went wholly out of sight.

When all was still, Bannertail made his way to the broken mushroom; rosy
red and beautiful its cap, snowy white its stem and its crisp, juicy flesh.

But of this he took no count. The smelling of it was his great chemic test. It
had the quaint, earthy odor of the little ones he had seen before, and yet a
pungent, food-like smell, like butternuts, indeed, with the sharp pepper
tang of the rind a little strong, and a whiff, too, of the many-legged
crawling things that he had learned to shun. Still, it was alluring as food.
And now was a crucial time, a veritable trail fork. Had Bannertail been fed
and full, the tiny little sense of repulsion would have turned the scale,
would have reasserted and strengthened the first true verdict of his
guides — "Bad, let it alone." But it had an attractive nut-like aroma that was
sweetly appetizing, that set his mouth a-watering; and this thing turned the
scale — he was hungry.

He nibbled and liked it, and nibbled yet more. And though it was a big,
broad mushroom, he stopped not till it all was gone. Food, good food it
surely was. But it was something more; the weird juices that are the earth-
child's blood entered into him and set the fountains of his life force playing
with marvellous power. He was elated. He was full of fight. He flung out a
defiant "Qua!" at a Hen-hawk flying over. He rummaged through the pines
to find that fighting Redsquirrel. He leaped tree gaps that he would not at
another time have dared. Yes, and he fell, too; but the ample silver plume

behind was there to land him softly on the earth. He made a long, far, racing journey, saw hills and woods that were new to him. He came to a big farmhouse like the one his youth had known, but passed it by, and galloped to another hillside. From the top of a pine he vented his wild spirits in a boisterous song—the song of spring and fine weather, and the song of autumn time and vigor.

The sun was low when, feeling his elation gone, feeling dumb and drowsy, indeed, he climbed the homestead tree and glided into the old Hawk nest to curl in his usual place beside his family.

Silvergray sniffed suspiciously; she smelled his whiskers, she nibble-nibbled with tongue and lips at the odd-smelling specks of whitish food on his coat, and the juices staining his face and paws. New food; it was strange, but pleased her not. A little puzzled, she went to sleep, and Bannertail's big tail was coverlet for all the family.

CHAPTER XXVI

THE ADDICT

HE sun came up, with its joyous wakening of the woods. All the Squirrel world was bright and alert—all but one. Mother went forth to the sun-up meal, Brownhead went rollicking forth, and Nyek-nyek went gliding, too. But Bannertail lay still. He had no words to state his case; he did not know that he had a case to state. He only knew that he was dull and sad, and did not feel the early morning call of joy. The juices of his weird feast were dried on paws and head, and the smell of them, though faint, was nauseating to him.

He did not move that day; he had no desire to move. The sun was low when at length he went forth and down. At the crystal spring he drank deep and drank again. Silvergray licked his fur when he came back with the youngsters to the nest. He was better now, and next sun-up was himself again, the big, boisterous, rollicking Squirrel of the plumy tail, the playmate of the young ones, the husband of his wife. And their merry lives went on, till one morning, on the bank of the creek that flowed from the high hill-country, he found a tiny, shiny fragment of the weird spellbinding mushroom. A table scrap, no doubt, flood-borne from a Redhead feast. He sniffed, as he sniffed all new, strange things. A moon back it would have been doubtful or repellent, but he had closed his ears to the first warning of the inner guide; so the warning now was very low. He had yielded to the slight appetite for this weird taste, so that appetite was stronger. He eagerly gobbled the shining, broken bit, and, possessed of keen desire for more, went bounding and pausing and fluffing, farther, farther off, nor stopped till once more high in the hill-country, among the pines and the banks where the toadstools of black magic grew.

Very keen was Bannertail when he swung from the overhead highway of the pines to the ground, to gallop over banks with nose alert. Nor had he far to go. This was toadstool time, and a scattered band of these embodied earth-sprites was spotting a sunlit bank with their smooth and blushing caps.

Was there in his little soul still a warning whisper? Yes. Just a little, a final, feeble "Beware, touch it not!"—very faint compared with the first-time warning, and now to be silenced by counter-doings, just as a single trail in the sand is wholly blotted out by a later trail much used that goes counterwise across it.

Just a little pause made he, when the sick smell of the nearest toadstool was felt and measured by his nose. The lust for that strong foody taste was overdominating. He seized and crunched and revelled in the flowing juices and the rank nut taste, the pepper tang, the toothsome mouthiness, and gobbled with growing unreined greed, not one, but two or three—he gorged on them; and though stuffed and full, still filled with lust that is to hunger what wounding is to soft caress. He rushed from one madcap toadstool to another, driving in his teeth, revelling in their flowing juices, like the blood of earthy gnomes, and rushed for joy up one tall tree after another. Then, sensing the Redsquirrels, pursued them in a sort of berserker rage, eager for fight, desperate fight, any fight, fight without hate, that would outlet his dangerous, boiling power, his overflow of energy. Joy and power were possessing his small brain and lusty frame. He found another bank of madcap cups; he was too gorged to eat them, but he tossed and chewed the juicy cups and stems. He raced after a fearsome Water-snake on a sunny bank, and, scared by the fury of his onslaught, the Snake slipped out of sight. He galloped up a mighty pine-tree, on whose highest limbs were two great Flickers, clacking. He chased them recklessly, then, clinging to a bark flake that proved loose, he was launched into the air, a hundred feet to fall. But his glorious tail was there to serve, and it softly let him down to earth. It was well for him that he met no cat or dog that day, for the little earth-born demon in his soul had cast out fear as well as wisdom.

And Mother Carey must have wept as she saw this very dear one take into his body and his brain a madness that would surely end his life. She loved him, but far more she loved his race. And just a little longer she would wait, and give him yet one chance. And if he willed not to be strong, then must he pay the price.

Not happy was his homecoming that night. Silvergray sniffed at his whiskers. She liked not his breath. There was no kindness in her voice, her only sound a harsh, low "Grrrff!"

And the family life went on.

CHAPTER XXVII

THE DREGS OF THE CUP

UT next morning! Why should it be told? It was as before, but far worse. So high as the peak is above the plain, so far is the plain below the peak. A crushed and broken Bannertail it was that lay enfeebled in the nest next day when the family went forth to feed and frolic.

Not that day did he go out, or wish to go. Sick unto death was he; so sick he did not care. The rest let him alone. They did not understand, and there was something about him which made them keep away. Next day he crawled forth slowly and drank at the spring. That day he lay on the sunning dray and ate but little. More than one sun arose and set before he was again the strong, hale, hearty Bannertail, the father of his family, the companion and protector of his wife.

CHAPTER XXVIII

THE WAY OF DESTRUCTION

HE little mother did not understand; she only had a growing sense of distrust, of repulsion, and an innate hatred of that strange complexity of smells. The children did not understand, but something there was about their father these times that made them much afraid.

They knew only the sorrow of it. They had no knowledge of how it came or how to prevent its coming. But big and everywhere is the All-Mother, Mother Carey, the wise one who seeks to have her strong ones build the race. Twice had she warned him. Now he should have one more chance.

The Thunder-moon, July, was dominating Jersey woods, when the lusty life force of the father Graycoat inevitably sent him roving to the woods of the madcaps. Plenty they were now, and many had been stored by the Redsquirrels for winter use, for this is the riddle of their being, that the Redsquirrels long ago have learned. On the bank, when they are rooted in the earth, their juices from the underworld are full of diabolic subtlety, are tempting in the mouth as they are deadly in the blood and sure destruction at the last. They must be uprooted, carried far from the ground and the underground, and high hung in the blessed purifying pine tops, where Father Sun can burn away their evil. There, after long months of sun and wind and rain purgation, their earth-born bodies are redeemed, are wholesome Squirrel food. This was the lesson Mother Carey had taught the Redheads, for their country is the country of the fool-trap toadstools. But the Graycoats know it not. And Bannertail came again.

CHAPTER XXIX

MOTHER CAREY'S LASH

HE wise men tell us that it is the same as the venom of Snakes. They tell us that it comes when the fool-trap toadstool is grown stale, and by these ye may know its hidden presence: When the cap is old and upturned at the edge, when hell-born maggots crawl and burrow and revel in the stem, when drops of gummy, poisonous yellow blood ooze forth, when both its smells — the warning smell of the crawling hundred-legger and the alluring smell of strong green butternuts — are multiplied to fourfold power.

Their day was nearly over. They were now like old worn hags, whose beauty is gone, and with it their power to please — hags who have become embittered and seek only to destroy. So the fool-trap toadstools waited, silently as hunters' deadfalls wait, until the moment comes to strike.

It was the same sweet piny woods, the same bright sparkling stream, and the Song-hawk wheeled and sang the same loud song, as Bannertail came once again to seek his earth-born food, to gratify his growing lust.

And Mother Carey led him on.

Plentifully strewn were the unholy madcaps, broad bent and wrinkled now, their weird aroma stronger and to a morbid taste more alluring. Even yet a tiny warning came as he sniffed their rancid, noxious aura. The nut allurement, too, was strong, and Bannertail rejoiced.

The feast was like the other, but shorter, more restrained. There were little loathsome whiffs and acrid hints that robbed it of its zest. Long before half a meal, the little warden that dwells somewhere betwixt mouth and maw began to send offensive messages to his brain, and even with a bite between his teeth there set in strong a fearful devastating revulsion, a climax of disgust, a maw-revolt, an absolute loathing.

His mouth was dripping with its natural juice, something gripped his throat, the last morsel was there and seemed to stick. He tight closed his eyes, violently shook his head. The choking lump was shaken out. Pains shot through his body. Limbs and lungs were cramped. He lay flat on the bank with head down-hill. He jerked his head from side to side with violent insistence. His stomach yielded most of the fateful mass. But the poison had entered into his body, already was coursing in his veins.

Writhing with agony, overwhelmed with loathing, he lay almost as dead, and the smallest enemy he ever had might now and easily have wreaked the limit of revenge. It was accident so far as he was concerned that made him crawl into a dense thicket and like dead to lie all that day and the night and the next day. And dead he would have been but for the unusual vigor of his superb body. Good Mother Carey kept his enemies away.

Back at the home nest the mate and family missed him, not much or pointedly, as would folk of a larger brain and life, but they missed him; and from the tall, smooth shaft that afternoon the little mother sent a long "qua" call. But there was no answering "qua." She had no means of knowing; she had no way of giving help had she known.

The sun was low on Jersey hills that second day when poor broken Bannertail, near-dead Bannertail, came to himself, his much-enfeebled self. His head was throbbing, his body was cramped with pain, his mouth was dry and burning. Down-hill he crawled and groped slowly to the running stream and drank. It revived him a little, enough so he could crawl up the bank and seek a dry place under a log to lie in peace—sad, miserable, moaning peace.

Three days he suffered there, but the fever had turned on that first night; from the moment of that cooling drink he was on the mend. For food he had no wish, but daily and deeply he drank at the stream.

On that third day he was well enough to scramble up the hill; he passed a scattering group of the earthy madcaps. Oh, how he loathed them; their very smell set his mouth a-dripping, refusing its own proper juice.

Good things there were to eat on the ground, but he had little appetite, though for three days he had not eaten. He passed by fat white grubs and even nuts, but when he found some late wild strawberries he munched them eagerly. Their acid sweetness, their fragrant saneness, were what his poor sick body craved. He rested, then climbed a leaning tree. He had not strength for a real climb. In an old abandoned Flicker hole he curled himself in safety, and strong, gentle Mother Nature, Mother Carey, loving ever the brave ones that never give up, now spread her kindly influence, protecting, round about him and gave him blessed, blessed sleep.

CHAPTER XXX

HIS AWAKENING

T was late on that fourth day when Bannertail awoke. He was a little better now. He slowly went down that tree, tail first; very sick, indeed, is a Squirrel when he goes down a tree tail first. Sweet, cooling water was his need, and again a fragrant meal of the tonic strawberries; then back to the tree.

Next day he was up with the morning Robins, and now was possessed of the impulse to go home. Vague pictures of his mate and little ones, and the merry home tree, came on his ever-clearer brain. He set out with a few short hops, as he used to go, and, first sign of sanity, he stopped to fluff his tail. He noticed that it was soiled with gum. Nothing can dethrone that needful basic instinct to keep in order and perfect the tail. He set to work and combed and licked each long and silvered hair; he fluffed it out and tried its billowy beauty, and having made sure of its perfect trim he kept on, cleaned his coat, combed it, went to the brook-side and washed his face and paws clean of every trace of that unspeakable stuff, and in the very cleansing gave himself new strength. Sleek and once more somewhat like himself he was, when on he went, bounding homeward with not short bounds, but using every little lookout on the way to peer around and fluff and jerk his tail.

Back at the home tree at last, nearly seven suns had come and gone since the family had seen him.

The first impulse of the little mother was hostility. A stranger is always a hostile in the woods. But he flicked the white flag on his tail tip, and slowly climbed the tree. The youngsters in alarm had hidden in the nest at mother's "Chik, chik." She came cautiously forward. His looks were familiar yet strange. Here now was the time to use caution. He swung up nearly to the door. She stood almost at bay, uttered a little warning "Ggrrrfffhh." He crawled up closer. She spread her legs, clutched firmly on the bark above him. He wigwagged his silver tail-tip and, slowly drawing nearer, reached out. Their whiskers met; she sniffed, smell-tested him. No question now. A little changed, a little strange, but this was surely her mate. She wheeled and went into the nest. He came more slowly after, put in his head, gave a low, soft "Er." There was no reply and no hostile move. He crawled right in, his silver plume was laid about them all, and the reunited family slept till the hour arrived for evening meal.

CHAPTER XXXI

THE UNWRITTEN LAW

HIS is the law of the All-Mother, the more immovable because unwritten; this is the law of surfeit.

Many foods there are which are wholesome, except that they have in them a measure of poison.

For these the All-Mother has endowed the wild things' bodies with a subtle antidote, which continues self-replenishing so long as the containing flask is never wholly emptied. But if it so chance that in some time of fearful stress the flask is emptied, turned upside down, drained dry, it never more will fill. The small alembic that distils it breaks, as a boiler bursts if it be fired while dry. Thenceforth the toxin that it overcame has virulence and power; that food, once wholesome, is a poison now.

A "surfeit" men call this breaking of the flask; all too well is it known. By this, unnumbered healthful foods—strawberries, ice-cream, jam, delicate meat, eggs, yes, even simple breads can by the devastating drain of one rash surfeit be turned into very foods of death. The poison always was there, but the secret, neutralizing chemical is gone, the elixir is destroyed, and by the working of the law its deadly power is loosed. As poor second now to this lost and subtle protection, the All-Mother endows the body with another, one of a lower kind. She makes that food so repellent to the unwise, punished creature that he never more desires it. She fills him with a fierce repulsion, the bodily rejection that men call "nausea."

This is the law of surfeit. Bannertail had fallen foul of it, and Mother Carey, loving him as she ever loves her strong ones, had meted out the fullest measure of punishment that he, with all his strength, could bear and yet come through alive.

The Red Moon of harvest was at hand. The Graycoat family was grown, and happy in the fulness of their lives, and Bannertail was hale and filled with the joy of being alive, leading his family beyond old bounds, teaching them the ways of the farther woods, showing them new foods that the season brings. He, wise leader now, who once had been so unwise. Then Mother Carey put him to the proof. She led, he led them farther than they had ever gone before, to the remotest edge of the hickory woods. On a bank half sunlit as they scampered over the leaves and down the logs, he found a blushing, shining gnome-cap, an earth-born madcap. Yes, the very same, for in this woods they came, though they were rare. One whiff, one identifying sniff of that Satanic exhalation, and Bannertail felt a horrid clutching at his throat, his lips were quickly dripping, his belly heaved, he gave a sort of spewing, gasping sound, and shrank back from that shining cap with eyes that bulged in hate, as though he saw a Snake. There is no way of fully telling his bodily revulsion. The thing that once was so alluring, was so loathsome that he could not stand its fetid odor on the wind. And the young ones were caught by the unspoken horror of the moment, they took it in; they got the hate sense. They tied up that horror in their memories with that rank and sickly smell. They turned away, Bannertail to drink in the running brook, to partly forget in a little while, yet never quite to forget. He was saved, the great All-Mother had saved him, which was a good thing, but not in itself a great thing. This was the great thing, that in that moment happened — the loathing of the earth-born fiend was implanted in his race, and through them would go on to bless his generations yet to be.

CHAPTER XXXII

SQUIRREL GAMES

AMES are used among wild animals for the training of the young. King of the castle, tag, hide-and-seek, follow-my-leader, catch-as-catch-can, wrestling, coasting, high-dive, and, in rare cases, even ball games are enjoyed. Most of them were in some sort played by the young Squirrels. But these are world-wide, they had one or two that were peculiarly their own, and of these the most exciting was the dangerous game of "teasing the Hawk."

Three kinds of big Hawks there are in the Squirrel woods in summertime: the Hen-hawk that commonly sails high in the air, screaming or whistling, and that at other times swoops low and silent through the woods, and always is known by his ample wings and bright red tail; the gray Chicken-hawk that rarely soars, but that skims among the trees or even runs on the ground, whose feathers are gray-brown, and whose voice is a fierce crek, crek, creek; and the Song-hawk or Singer, who is the size of the Chicken-hawk, but a harmless hunter of mice and frogs, and known at all seasons by the stirring song that he pours out as he wheels like a Skylark high in the blue.

The inner guide had warned the boisterous Bannertail to beware of all of them. Experience taught him that they will attack, and yet are easily baffled, if one does but slip into a hole or thicket, or even around the bole of a tree.

Many times that summer did Bannertail avoid the charge of Redtail or Chicken-hawk by the simple expedient of going through a fork or a maze of branches. There was no great danger in it, as long as he kept his head; and it did not disturb him, or cause his heart a single extra beat. It became a regular incident in his tree-top life, just as a stock man is accustomed to the daily danger of a savage Bull, but easily eludes any onset by slipping through a fence. It does not cause him a tremor, he is used to it; and men there are who make a sport of it, who love to tease the Bull, who enjoy his helpless rage as he vainly tries to follow. His mighty strength is offset by their cunning and agility. It is a pretty match, a very ancient game, and never quite loses zest, because the Bull does sometimes win; and then there is one less Bull-teaser on the stock-range.

This was the game that Bannertail evolved. Sure of himself, delighting in his own wonderful agility, he would often go out to meet the foe, if he saw the Hen-hawk or the Chicken-hawk approaching. He would flash his silver tail, and shrill "Grrrff, grrrff," by way of challenge.

The Hen-hawk always saw. "Keen-eyed as a hawk" is not without a reason. And, sailing faster than a driving leaf, he would swish through the hickory woods to swoop at the challenging Squirrel. But just as quick was Bannertail, and round the rough trunk he would whisk, the Hawk, rebounding in the air to save himself from dashing out his brains or being impaled, would now be greeted on the other side by the head and flashing tail of the Squirrel, and another with loud, defiant "Ggrrrffhh, grggrrrffhh."

Down again would swoop the air bandit, quicker than a flash, huge black claws advanced, and Bannertail would wait tillthe very final instant, rejoicing in his every nerve at tension, and just as those deadly grappling-irons of the Hawk were almost at his throat, he would duck, the elusive, baffling tail would flash in the Hawk's very face, and the place the Graycoat had occupied on the trunk was empty. The grapnels of the Hawk clutched only bark; and an instant later, just above, the teasing head and the flaunting tail of Bannertail would reappear, with loudly voiced defiance.

The Hawk, like the Bull, is not of gentle humor. He is a fierce and angry creature, out to destroy; his anger grows to fury after such defeat, he is driven wild by the mockery of it, and oftentimes he begets such a recklessness that he injures himself by accident, as he charges against one of the many sharp snags that seem ever ready for the Squirrel-kind's defense.

Yes, a good old game it is, with the zest of danger strong. But there is another side to it all.

CHAPTER XXXIII

WHEN BANNERTAIL WAS SCARRED FOR LIFE

T makes indeed merry play, with just enough of excitement when you bait the Bull, and dodge back to the fence to laugh at his impotent raging. But it makes a very different chapter when a second Bull comes on the other side of the fence. Then the game is over, the Bull-baiter must find some far refuge or scramble up the nearest sheltering tree, or pay the price.

Bannertail had an ancient feud with the big Hen-hawk, whose stick nest was only a mile away, high in a rugged beech. There were a dozen farmyards that paid unwilling tribute to that Hawk, a hundred little meadows with their Mice and Meadowlarks, and one open stretch of marsh with its Muskrats and its Ducks. But the hardwood ridges, too, he counted on for dues. The Squirrels all were his, if only he could catch them. Many a game had he and Bannertail, a game of life and death.

They played again that morning in July. It was the same old swooping of the whistling pinions, and the grasping of strong yellow feet with hard black claws, grasping at nothing, where was a Graycoat half a heartbeat back, the same flaunting silver flag, the mocking "Grrrff, grrrff," the teasing and daring of the Hawk to make another swoop. Then did that big Hen-hawk what he should have done before. He filled the air with his war-cry, the long screaming "Yek-yek-yeeeek!" Coursing low and swift came another, his mate, the lady bandit, even fiercer than himself. Swift and with little noise she came. And when savage old Yellow-eyes swooped and Bannertail whisked around the tree, he whisked right into the clutches of the deadlier she-one. He barely escaped by a marvellous side rush around the trunk. Here again was Yellow-eyes, but right in his face Bannertail dashed his big silvery tail. The Hawk in his haste clutched at its nothingness, or he would have got the Graycoat. But luck was with Bannertail, and again he dodged around the trunk. Alas, the she Hawk was there, and struck; her mighty talons grazed his haunch, three rips they made in his glossy, supple coat. In an instant more the Redtail would have trussed him, for there was no cover, only the big, outstanding trunk, with the Hen-hawks above and below. A moment more and Bannertail's mate, helpless in the distant nest, would have seen him borne away. But as they closed, he leaped—leaped with all his strength, far from them into open air, and faster than they could fly in such a place, down, down, his silver plume in function just behind him, down a hundred feet to fall and land in a thicket of laurel, wounded and bleeding, but safe. He scrambled into a thicker maze, and gazed with new and tenser feelings at the baffled Hen-hawks, circling, screaming high above him.

Soon the bandits gave up. Clearly the Graycoat had won, and they flew to levy their robber-baron tribute on some others that they held to be their vassals.

Yes, Bannertail had won, by a narrow lead. He had taken a mighty hazard and had learned new wisdom—Never play the game with death till you have to, for if you win one hundred times and lose once you have lost your whole stake. On his haunch he carried, carries yet, the three long scars, where the fur is a little paler—the brand of the robber baroness, the slash of the claws that nearly got him.

Have you noted that in the high Alleghenies, where the Graycoats seldom see hunters of any kind, they scamper while the enemy is far away; but they peer from upper limbs and call out little challenges? In Jersey woods, where a wiser race has come, they never challenge a near foe; they make no bravado rushes. They signal if they see an enemy near, then hide away in perfect stillness till that enemy, be it Hawk in air or Hound on earth, is far away, or in some sort ceases to be a menace.

And menfolk hunters, who tell of their feats around the glowing stove in the winter-time, say there is a new race of Graycoats come. Any gunner could kill one of the old sort, but it takes a great hunter such as themselves to get one of the new. This latter-day Graycoat has gotten much wisdom into his little brain, and one of the things he knows: "It never pays to gamble with destruction."

The new race, they say, began in a certain hickory wood. We know that wood, and we have seen a little how the wisdom came, and can easily reason why it spread.

CHAPTER XXXIV

THE FIGHT WITH THE BLACK DEMON

EXT in importance to the Squirrels, after the towering trees with their lavish bounty, was the brook that carried down scraps of the blue sky to inlay them with green moss, purple logs, and gold-brown stones, that sang its low, sweet song both day and night, and that furnished to the family their daily drink.

"Do not drink at the pond" is a Squirrel maxim, for in it lurks the fearful Snapping Turtle and the grinning Pike. Its banks are muddy, too, and the water warm. It is better to drink from some low log, along the brook itself.

And do not drink in the blinding sunlight, which makes it hard to see if danger is near; then, too, it is that the Blacksnake crawls out to seek some basking place in the hottest sun.

Yes, this is Squirrel wisdom; the morning drink is at sunrise, the evening at sunset, when the cool shade is on the woods but darkness not begun.

The Graycoat family held together still, though the Harvest-moon was red in the low eastern sky. Some Squirrel families break up as soon as the young are nearly grown. But some there are that are held together longer, very long, by unseen bonds of sympathy with which they have been gifted in a little larger measure than is common. Brownhead was much away, living his own life. Still, he came home. Nyek-nyek, gentle, graceful Nyek-nyek, clung to her mother and the old nest, like a very weanling; and rest assured that in Squirrel-land, as in others, love is begotten and intensified by love.

The morning drink and the morning meal were the established daily routine. Then came a time of exercise and play. But all Squirrels that are hale and wise take a noonday nap.

Each was stretched on one or other of the sleeping platforms, lying lazily at ease one noontime. The day was very hot, and the sun swung round so it glared on Nyek-nyek's sleeping-porch. Panting soon with the heat, she decided to drink, swung to the gangway of their huge trunk and started down the tree. The little mother, ever alert, watched the young one go. There was in her heart just a shadow of doubt, of distrust, much as a human mother might feel if she saw her toddler venture forth alone into the night.

Nyek-nyek swung to the ground, coursed in billowy ripples of silver-gray along a log, stopped on a stump to look around and religiously fluff her tail, while mother dreamily watched through half-closed eyes. Then out into the brilliant sunlight she went. Some creatures are dazed and made lazy by the hot, bright glare, some find in it a stimulant, a multiplier of their life force; it sets their senses on a keener edge; it gifts them with new speed, intensifies their every power.

The Graycoats are of the first kind, and of the second was Coluber, the long, black, shiny, blue-black Snake that was lying like a limp and myriad-linked chain flung across a big, low log — a log that sucked the sun heat as it lay, just where the brook expanded to the pond. Never a blink was there in those gray-green eyes, never a quiver in that long, lithe tongue. One not knowing would have said he is dead; one knowing him well would havesaid he is filling up his storage-batteries to the full. Never a wriggle was there in even the nervous tail tip, that nearly always switches to and fro; yet not a move of the Squirrel since she left her sleeping porch was lost on him.

What was it gave a new pathway to the young Graycoat? Was it Mother Carey who led her with a purpose? Not to the familiar log she went, where the family had always found an ideal footing when they took the morning drink, but down-stream, toward the pond and on to the little muddy shore.

The mother Squirrel saw that, and her feeling of doubt grew stronger. She rose up to follow, but gazed a moment to see a sudden horror. Just as the little Nyek-nyek stooped and sank her face deep to her eyes in the cooling flood, the Blacksnake sprang, sprang from his coil as a Blacksnake springs, when the victim is within the measured length. Sprang with his rows of teeth agape, clinched on her neck, and in a trice the heavy coils, tense with energy, ridged with muscle, flash-lapped around her neck and loins, gripped in an awful grip, while the lithe, live scaly tail wrapped round a branch to anchor both killer and victim to the place. One shriek of "Qua," another fainter, and a final gasp, and no more sound from Nyek-nyek. But she struggled, a hopeless, helpless struggle. The mother saw it all. Fear of that terrible Snake was forgotten. Not one moment did she pause. She did not clamber down that tree. She leaped to the next and a lower yet, and along a log; five heart-beats put her on the spot; and with all her force she drove her teeth into the hard, scaly coil of the beast that she held in mortal fear. With a jerk the monster quit his neck hold on the young one. She was helpless, bound in his coil, and the Snake's dread jaws with the rows of pointed teeth clamped on the mother's neck, and another fold of that long, hellish length was hitched around her throat. Scratch she could and struggle, but bite she could not, for the coil held her as in a vise. For a moment only could she make a sound, the long, long, screaming "Queeee," the Squirrel call for help; and Bannertail, lazily dozing on his sunning perch, sprang up and set his ears acock.

It was not repeated, but the sound of struggle was there, and the keen-eyed father Squirrel saw the flash of a silver tail, the signal of his kind. And from that perch high in the air he leaped in one long, parachuting leap; he landed on the ground, and in three mighty bounds he was at the place. The horror of the Snake was on him. It set his coat a-bristling; but it did not hold him back. It only added desperation to his onset. Clutching that devilish scaly neck with both his arms, he drove in his chisel teeth and ground them in, down to the very bone, as Silvergray could not have done. He worked and tugged and stabbed again, and the Snake, sensing a new and stronger foe, relaxed on Silvergray, snapped with his hateful jaws, seized Bannertail's strong shoulder just where he best could stand it— where the skin is thick and strong the Blacksnake drove in and gripped. And Bannertail, as quick, quit his first hold on the coil that was strangling Nyek-nyek, and by good luck, or maybe by better wisdom than his own, drove, fighting fierce, into the demon's throat, the weak spot in that scaly armor. Deep sank the Squirrel's teeth, and pangs of mortal agony went thrilling through the reptile's length. But he was strong, and a desperate fighter, too. The coils unloosed on the senseless form of Nyek-nyek and lapped in a trice on Bannertail, three times round, straining, crushing, while his rows of cruel fangs were sunk in the Squirrel's silvery side.

But in throwing all his force against Bannertail he released the little Gray mother. She flung herself again on the black horror, and bit with all her power the head that was gripped on the shoulder of her mate. Very narrow is the demon reptile's head, and only one place was open, offered to her grip. She bit with all her force across the eyes, her long, sharp chisels entered in. His eyes were pierced, his brain was stung. With an agonizing last convulsion he wrenched on Bannertail, then, quivering with a palsy that changed to a springing open of the coils, he dashed his head from side to side, lashed his tail, heaved this way and that, coiled up, then straightened out. The Squirrels leaped back, the monsterlashed in writhing convolutions, felt the cool water that he could no longer see, went squirming out upon it, working his frothy jaws, lashing, thrashing with his tail. Then up from the darkest depths came a hideous goggle-eyed head, a monstrous head, as big as a Squirrel's whole body, and on it a horny beak, which, opening, showed a huge red maw, and the squirming Blacksnake was seized by the bigger brute. Crushed and broken in those mighty jaws was the Black One's supple spine; torn open by those great claws was his belly, ended was his life. The Snapper sank, taking the Blacksnake with him. It was the finish of an ancient feud between them, and down in the dark depths of the pond the Water Demon feasted on the body of his foe.

And Bannertail, the brave fighter, with the heroic little Mother and Nyek-nyek now revived, drew quickly back to safety. A little cut they were, but mostly breathless, their very wind squeezed out by those dread coils. The ripples on the pool had scarcely died before they were all three again in the dear old nest, with Brownhead back anew from a far journey. Without words, were they to tell of their thrills and fears, or their joy; but this reaction came: They cuddled up in the nest, a little closer than before, a little more at one, a little less to feel the scatteration craze that comes in most wild families when the young are grown; which meant these young will have for a little longer the good offices of their parents, and are thereby fitted a little better for the life-battle, a little more likely to win.

Is it not by such accumulating little things that brain and brawn and the world success of every dominating race of creatures has been built?

CHAPTER XXXV

THE PROPERTY LAW AMONG ANIMALS

HAT was the year of the wonderful nut crop. It is commonly so; the year of famine is followed by one of plenty. Red oaks and white were laden, as well as the sweet shag hickories. And the Bannertail family in their grove watched with a sort of owner pride the thick green hanging clusters of their favorite food.

Like small boys too eager to await the baking of their cake, nibbling at the unsatisfactory half-done dough, they cut and opened many a growing nut. Its kernel, very small as yet, was good; but the rind, oozing its green-brown juices, stained their jaws and faces, yes, — their arms and breasts, till it was hard to recognize each other in these dark-brown masks. For the disfigurement they cared nothing. Only when the thick sap, half drying, gummed his silvery plume, did Bannertail abandon other pursuits to lick and clear and thoroughly comb that priceless tail; and what he did, the others, by force of his energetic example, were soon compelled to do.

The Hunting-moon, September, came. The nuts were fully grown but very green. "Who owns the nuts?" is an old question in the woods. Usually they are owned by the one who can possess them effectively, although there are some restraining, unwritten laws.

Squirrels have three well-marked ideas of property. First, of the nesting-place which they have possessed, and the nest which they have built; second, the food which they have found or stored; third, the range which is their homeland — the boundaries of which are not well-defined — but most jealously held against those of their own kind. The Homeland is also held against all who eat their foods so that it is part of the food-property sense. All three were strong in Bannertail; and his growing pride in the coming nut yield was much like that of a farmer who, by the luck of good weather, is blessed with a bumper crop of corn.

It seemed as though word of the coming feast had spread to other and far-off places, for many other nut-eaters kept drifting that way, turning up in the hickory woods that the Graycoats thought their own.

The Bluejay and the Redheaded Woodpecker came. They pecked long and hard at the soggy husks to get at the soft, sweet, milk-white meat. They did little damage, for their beaks were not strong enough to twist off the nuts and carry them away, but the Graycoats felt that these were poachers and drove them off. Of course it was easy for the birds to keep out of reach, but they hovered about, stealing—yes, that was what the Squirrels thought about it—stealing the hickory harvest when they could.

Then came other poachers, the Redsquirrel with his mate, cheeky, brazen-fronted, aggressive as usual; they would come quietly, when the Graycoats were asleep or elsewhere, and proceed to cut the nut bunches. Many times the only notice of their presence was the sudden "thump, thump" of the nut bunch striking the ground after the Red One had cut it loose. His intention had been to go down quietly after it, split the husks, and carry off the luscious, half-ripe nuts to his storehouse. But the racket called the Graycoats' attention. Bannertail and Brownhead would rush forth like settlers to fight off an Indian raid, or like householders to save their stuff from burglars.

There was little actual fighting to do with the Red Ones, for they had learned to fear and fly from the Graycoats, but they did not fly far. Their safest refuge was a hole underground, where Graycoats could not or would not follow, and after waiting for quiet the Red Robber would come out again, and sometimes, at least, get away with a load of the prized nuts.

New enemies approached one day, nothing less than other Graycoats, some Squirrels of their own kind, travelling from some other land, travelling, maybe, like Joseph and his brethren, away from a place of famine, till now they found an Egypt, a land of plenty.

Against them Bannertail went vigorously to war. It is well known that the lawful owner fights more valiantly, with more heart, with indomitable courage indeed, while the invader is in doubt. He lacks the backing of a righteous cause. He half expects to be put to flight, even as he goes forth to battle. And the Bannertails were able to make good their claims to the hickory grove. Yet it kept them ever alert, ever watchful, ever ready to fight.

Partly because the nuts were already good food, and partly because it kept others from stealing them, the Graycoats cut some of the crop in September.

CHAPTER XXXVI

GATHERING THE GREAT NUT HARVEST

N the Leaf-falling-moon, October, the husks began to dry and split, and the nuts to fall of themselves. Then was seen a wild, exciting time, the stirring of habits and impulses laid in the foundations of the race.

No longer wabbly or vague, as in that first autumn, but fully aroused and dominating was the instinct to gather and bury every precious, separate nut. Bannertail had had to learn slowly and partly by seeing the Redsquirrels making off with the prizes. But he had learned, and his brood had the immediate stimulus of seeing him and their mother at work; and because he was of unusual force, it drove him hard, with an urge that acted like a craze. He worked like mad, seizing, stripping, smelling, appraising, marking, weighing every nut he found.

What, weighing it? Yes, every nut was weighed by the wise harvester. How? By delicate muscular sense. It was held for a moment between the paws, and if it seemed far under weight it was cast aside as worm-eaten, empty, worthless; if big, but merely light in weight, that meant probably a fat worm was within. Then that nut was split open and the worm devoured. A wormy nut was never stored. If the nut was heavy, round, and perfect, the fine balance in the paws and the subtle sense of smell asserted the fact, and then it was owner-marked. How? By turning it round three times in the mouth, in touch with the tongue. This left the personal touch of that Squirrel on it, and would protect it in a measure from being carried off by other Graysquirrels, especially when food abounded. Then, rushing off several hops from the place where the last nut was buried, Bannertail would dig deep in the ground, his full arm's length, ram down the nut held in his teeth; then, pushing back the earth with snout and paws, would tamp that down, replacing the twigs and dry leaves so the nut was safely hidden. Then to the next, varying the exercise by dashing, not after the visiting Graysquirrels — they kept their distance — but after some thieving Chipmunk or those pestiferous Redsquirrels who sought sometimes to unearth his buried treasure. Or, he would dart noisily up the tree, to chase the Bluejays who were trying to rob them of the nuts not yet fallen; then back to earth again, where was his family—Silvergray, Brownhead, and Nyek-nyek—inspired by his example, all doing as he did, working like beavers, seizing, husking, weighing, marking, digging, dig-dig-digging and burying nuts all day long. Hundreds of these little graves they dug, till the ground under every parent tree was a living, crowded burying-ground of the tree's own children. Morning, noon, and evening they worked, as long as there was light enough to see.

A cool night and another drying day brought down another hickory shower. And the Graycoats worked without ceasing. They were tired out that night. They had driven off a score of robbers, they had buried at least a thousand nuts, each in a separate hole. The next day was an even more strenuous time. For seven full days they worked, and then the precious nut harvest was over. Acorns—red and white and yellow—might come later, and some be buried and some not. The Bluejays, Woodpeckers, and the Redsquirrels would get a handsome share, and pile them up in storehouses, a day's gathering in one place, for such is their way, but the hickory-nuts were the precious things that counted for the Bannertail brood. Ten thousand at least had the Graycoats buried, each an arm's length down, and deftly hidden, with the trash of the forest floor replaced.

This undoubtedly was their only impulse, to bury the rich nuts for future use as food. But Nature's plan was larger. There were other foods in the woods at this season. The Squirrels would not need the precious hickories for weeks or months; all sign that might mark the burial-place would be gone. When really driven by need the Squirrels would come and dig up these caches. Memory of the locality first, then their exquisite noses would be their guides. They would find most of the nuts again. But not all. Some would escape the diggers, and what would happen to these? They would grow. Yes, that was Nature's plan. The acorns falling and lying on the ground can burst their thin coats, send down a root and up a shoot at once, but the hickory must be buried or it will dry up before it grows. This is the hickory's age-old compact with the Graysquirrel: You bury my nuts for me, plant my children, and you may have ninety-five per cent of the proceeds for your trouble, so long only as you save the other five per cent and give them a chance to grow up into hickory-trees.

This is the unwritten but binding bargain that is observed each year. And this is the reason why there are hickory-trees wherever there are Graysquirrels. Where the Graycoats have died out the hickory's days are numbered. And foolish man, who slays the Graysquirrel in his reckless lust for killing, is also destroying the precious hickory-trees, whose timber is a mainstay of the nation-feeding agriculture of the world. He is like the fool on a tree o'erhanging the abyss, who saws the very limb on which depends his life.

CHAPTER XXXVII

AND TO-DAY

IS race still lives in Jersey woods; they have come back into their own. Go forth, O wise woodman, if you would become yet wiser. Go in the dew-time after rain, when the down, dry leaves have lost their tongues. Go softly as you may, you will see none of the Squirrel-kind, for they are better woodmen than you. But sit in silence for half an hour, so the discord of your coming may be forgotten.

Then a little signal, "Qua," like the quack of a Wild-duck, will be answered by the countersign, "Quaire"; then there will be wigwag signal flashes with silver tail-tips. "All's well!" is the word they are passing, and if you continue very discreet and kind, they will take up their lives again. The silent trees will give up dryad forms, not many, not hundreds, not even scores, but a dozen or more, and they will play and live their greenwood lives about you, unafraid. They will come near, if you still emanate unenmity, so you may see clearly the liquid eyes, the vibrant feelers on their legs and lips. And if these be tree-top wood-folk, very big and strong of their kind, with silvery coats and brownie caps, and tails that are of marvellous length and fluff, like puffs of yellow smoke with silver frills or flashes of a white light about them, then be sure of this, by virtue of the sleek, lithe beauty of their outer forms and the quick wood-wisdom of their little brains — you are watching a clan of Bannertail's own brood.

And, further, rest assured that when the hard nuts fall next autumn-time, Mother Carey has at hand a chosen band of planters for her trees, and a noble forest for another age will be planted on these hills, timber for all time.